GEMINI
SLEEPING DRAGONS BOOK 3

OPHELIA BELL

Gemini
Copyright © 2014 Ophelia Bell
Cover Art Designed by Dawné Dominique
Photograph Copyrights © Fotolio.com, DepositPhotos.com, CanStock.com

All rights reserved. No part of this book may be reproduced in any form or by any electronic means, including information storage and retrieval systems, without permission in writing from the author, except by a reviewer who may quote brief passages in review.

This is a work of fiction. Names, places, characters, and events are fictitious in every regard. Any similarities to actual events and persons, living or dead, is purely coincidental. Any trademarks, service marks, product names, or named features are assumed to be the property of their respective owners, and are used only for reference. There is no implied endorsement if any of these terms are used.

Published by Ophelia Bell
UNITED STATES

ISBN-13: 978-1544292892
ISBN-10: 1544292899

ALSO BY OPHELIA BELL

SLEEPING DRAGONS SERIES

Animus

Tabula Rasa

Gemini

Shadows

Nexus

Ascend

RISING DRAGONS SERIES

Night Fire
Breath of Destiny
Breath of Memory
Breath of Innocence
Breath of Desire
Breath of Love
Breath of Flame & Shadow
Breath of Fate
Sisters of Flame

IMMORTAL DRAGONS SERIES

Dragon Betrayed
Dragon Blues
Dragon Void

STANDALONE EROTIC TALES

After You
Out of the Cold

OPHELIA BELL TABOO

Burying His Desires

•

Blackmailing Benjamin
Betraying Benjamin
Belonging to Benjamin

•

Casey's Secrets
Casey's Discovery
Casey's Surrender

The best things come in pairs.

CHAPTER ONE

Dimtri's eyes popped open unbidden and he stared into the dim reaches of the dragon temple above him. He let his eyes and ears acclimate to being awake, ignoring the remnants of the dream he'd been having about his twin brother. *Alex... you should be here, too*, he thought.

This had been their shared dream, finding a place like this. The desire to find evidence that the mythical creatures were real had driven the two brothers through their studies. Now Dimitri was *there*, waking up to the image of exquisitely carved jade dragons that guarded every reach of the massive temple, and the only thing on his mind was the regret that Alex wasn't there to share it with him.

You're here to let that go. To let Alex go, he told himself as he clambered out of his sleeping bag and hunted for the kettle. The nearby fountain splashed and gurgled and Dimitri marveled at the artistry of the carvings that made up their water source while he filled the kettle. The strange stones that filled the firepit they used for cooking were even more fascinating, and yet another detail he could imagine Alex enthusing over. He set the kettle down onto the hot bed of glowing rocks and sat back. Unable to shake thoughts of his brother just yet, he gave in one more time to the memories that played out in the bright embers while he waited for the water to boil so he could make coffee.

"Hey, love. I'd like you to meet my brother, Dimitri."

Dimitri put on his brightest, most welcoming smile to greet his twin brother's girlfriend. "Thea. Alex has told me so much about you." *Probably a lot more than you'd be comfortable with*, he thought. Alex's description of her had definitely done her justice, at least.

He reached out his hands to clasp hers affectionately, acutely conscious of her soft skin and the way she filled out the sheer, black blouse she wore. He let his hands linger over hers just a little longer than necessary, ignoring the little voice in his head reminding him that she was taken.

She was petite and curvaceous, with short, curly brown hair. Pixieish was how Alex had described her the week before. "With luscious lips and a cunt that tastes like strawberries." Dimitri agreed that her lips did indeed appear luscious, and his brother was not prone to exaggeration so he trusted the other detail was accurate, too. If he didn't feel just a little desperate for attention after being dumped himself, he'd have been able to deal with the soft allure of a pretty girl. As it was, Thea was a little *too* perfect. Alex had good taste. They both did, but somehow Alex was the better judge of character.

"Wow, Dimitri, you are every bit as handsome as your brother told me," Thea replied with a flirty twinkle in her eye that made Dimitri curse his brother in response. She'd won him over already, and now she was flirting?

Dimitri pulled his hands back and shoved them in his pockets, taking her in surreptitiously while they walked to the bar. As first impressions went, his impression of Thea was good, at least objectively. Not that he could be strictly objective after thinking about her naked. But as long as he ignored his unmistakable attraction to her he could tell that Alex seemed happy, and his brother's happiness meant more to him than anything.

At the bar, the three of them bantered like best friends. After a few drinks Thea decided to make it her singular purpose to find Dimitri a date.

"I don't think my brother's looking for a date tonight, love," Alex told her.

"How do you know?" she asked.

Dimitri was entertained by her contrary tone. His brother had found a live one. Not exactly surprising, but it didn't help him remain objective.

"I know because we share those details with each other." Alex met his eyes and took a drink of his beer. He hadn't been lying, but the truth was the two of them shared everything. There was nothing Dimitri had experienced that Alex didn't know about. At least not yet.

Of course Alex was being cagey on purpose. It was an unspoken rule between the two of them that the secrets they shared with each other weren't meant for the ears of their lovers. Dimitri was still raw from a recent breakup. His brother knew all the sordid details of it, so it was unexpected that he'd have introduced Dimitri to a new flame so soon, knowing how sensitive he still was. Yet Alex had. So either Alex's relationship with this perfect woman was incredibly serious or something else was going on.

Dimitri took a long swallow of his beer, studying his brother through low-lidded eyes. *What have you got up your sleeve, brother?*

"Well, he looks lonely," Thea said. "And this place is *lousy* with pretty girls. He may not be as gorgeous as *you*, but it can't be that tough to find someone for him." She winked at Dimitri, obviously pleased with her joke. It wasn't the first time Dimitri had heard the joke—he'd even used it himself once or twice. Dimitri shared an amused glance with his brother, his mirror image, aside from their clothes, while Thea glanced around the room.

That first night set the tone for their interactions. Every Friday Dimitri would leave his tiny graduate assistant's office on campus, walk to the next wing to his brother's similar office, and they'd drive to meet Thea. Their destination was almost always the same comfortable little pub in the neighborhood where she lived.

Thea seemed to love hunting down girls for Dimitri, but after that first night it became clear it was just for show. Whether it was out of respect for him or because she started feeling some sense of possessiveness toward him, he couldn't be sure. She'd gotten into the habit of hooking her arms through both his and his brother's, and walking between them down the street. Dimitri thought she enjoyed some of the envious looks she'd get from other women, bookended by him and his brother as she was.

One pretty little pixie flanked by two Adonises was probably the trifecta of attractiveness. He almost wished he could be on the outside looking in, because the truth was nowhere near as interesting as what other people probably imagined.

Buzzed from her third drink, Thea laid a hand on Dimitri's arm. "Dimitri, it's been a month. Alex won't share no matter how much I beg. I think it's time you tell me exactly *what* this girl did to you. You've gotta get back on the horse, sweetie!"

"Thea…" Alex began, but Dimitri cut him off.

"No, it's fine. She's right—I should talk about it." He turned and met Thea's eager gaze. "Well, first of all it wasn't a girl."

Thea's eyes grew wide and she shot Alex a curious look before saying, "Oh God, why didn't you say something? I feel so dumb trying to hook you up with a girl. I'll switch focus, I have lousy gaydar, though…*clearly.*"

Dimitri laughed. "No, please. I don't need any help finding a date, and I actually *do* like girls, too. I'm just too busy focusing on my dissertation right now, I don't need the distraction." He took a deep breath and a long swallow of his beer, then let the rest of the story out in a rush just to get it over with. "That, and the person I'm getting over was my mentor so my life's about ten times as complicated as it needs to be." At least his mentor had prudently opted to take a sabbatical while the whole debacle blew over.

Dimitri was still nursing the painful humiliation of the disastrous affair. It never should have started, but it had. The ending had been epic and emotional. He was just grateful he had Alex to bolster his mood in the aftermath. And now that he'd told Thea, he found he was glad someone else was there to shoulder the burden. She reached out and gently squeezed his hand, then adroitly changed the subject. And that was that, at least he thought so.

Around midnight the three of them left, slightly the worse for wear after running into a group of other friends from the anthropology department where he and his brother were both finishing their masters degrees. Thea took up her customary spot between them and they headed haphazardly down the sidewalk toward her brownstone a few blocks away.

At her front steps he started to bid them both farewell and carry on alone back to the loft he shared with his brother. The place was depressingly lonely lately, so he'd most likely end up at the seedy dive bar nearby and close it down before going home to pass out.

Dimitri went in to hug Thea goodnight like always. Before he could react, her lips pressed against his, hot and sweet, and oh so welcome. His brain responded sluggishly at first, but other parts of him were much quicker on the uptake. His hands shifted down her back and pulled her closer before his actions registered.

"Thea, I…I think you got a little confused there," he said when he finally regained control and let go of her. "Alex is behind you. Honest mistake I guess." His stomach lurched when he met Alex's shocked gaze. His brother's look quickly faded, replaced by amused understanding. What the hell was Alex up to? What were they both up to?

"Nope," Thea said. "Not confused at all. Come inside with us, sweetie. Don't go home alone. Alex said you'd just go drink yourself silly anyway."

"Alex, what the fuck is going on?" Dimitri asked his brother. It was incredibly uncharacteristic for his twin to hide something like this.

"I would've warned you, but she wanted it to be spontaneous. Are you coming in or not?"

"You're telling me you planned this?" he asked, staring between them both, incredulous.

Thea appeared flushed and wide-eyed, but determined. "It was my idea, Dimitri. If you're not comfortable that's okay. Just come inside and at least talk about it, alright?"

He followed, not quite certain what he should expect. The kiss had confused him as much as it had turned him on, and incited a whole slew of questions. But there was no talking. Once through her door, she grabbed his hand and pulled him against her again. She kicked off her shoes and stood on bare tiptoes to reach him. The kiss was sweeter this time, now that he was expecting it, but he still had the strangest sense that he was trespassing somehow. He pulled away again, glancing at Alex for direction and to wordlessly confirm that he really wasn't crossing any lines.

"It's okay," Thea whispered. "Alex, tell him it's okay. Tell him I want you both. It's as much for me as it is for you, Dimitri." The exchange between the three of them was surreal. She kept her eyes locked on Dimitri's while talking to his brother.

Alex never said a single word. Instead, he led them both to the bedroom and paused by the bed, Thea facing him. He gave her a lust-filled, hungry look and captured her lips fiercely in his. The couple seemed to emanate desire and it only made Dimitri more uncertain what his role really was, particularly when Alex met his eyes over Thea's smaller figure. Dimitri didn't think he'd ever seen his brother look quite so lost to his libido, but then this was an aspect of their lives they'd never shared before.

"You sure you're okay with this?" Dimitri's throat constricted.

"Yeah…yeah I am." Blue eyes stared back at him, the mirror image of his own, but filled with a certainty Dimitri couldn't have managed even if he tried. His life had been one botched relationship after another for the last couple years, the latest just the cherry on top. Could he subsist on his brother's convictions?

He was still asking himself that question when Thea turned and leaned up on tiptoe to kiss him again. He closed his eyes and wrapped his arms around her, letting her press herself against him and tease her tongue deeper. She pulled away long enough to let Alex pull her shirt off over her head and unfasten her bra from behind. Her breasts were creamy and plump, tipped by hard, pink nipples. The urge to bend and suck them nearly overwhelmed him, but Dimitri was focused on getting her naked first.

Dimitri knelt and unfastened her jeans. He grazed his palms down her sides, pushing the denim down her hips along with the lacy panties she wore. Her narrow waist flared dramatically to her wide hips. His hands kept sliding down over her creamy thighs, the soft warmth making his palms tingle. She stood perfectly still while he explored skin as perfect and flawless as alabaster. He heard a sharp intake of breath when he grazed his fingertips along the juncture of her hip and pelvis, tracing the perfect little triangle of coarse, dark hair, trimmed to a point just above the cleft of her pussy. He glanced up and met her eyes, low-lidded and bright with desire. His eyes traveled beyond her face to his brother's blue-eyed stare, the wordless suggestion as clear to Dimitri as if his twin had spoken.

He leaned closer and captured the tip of one full breast between his teeth, pulling it between his lips and sucking until she moaned. With a gentle nudge from her, he stood again and enveloped her in his arms. Every lush curve of her seemed to brush against his arms, rub against his chest. She tugged at his t-shirt and they parted long enough for him to tear it off over his head while she hastily unbuckled his pants. Then she was on him again, kissing and moaning against his lips. His cock throbbed against the soft skin of her belly, the steady pulse reflecting the pounding of his heart. Christ, he wanted her so much. He wanted to be buried inside her deep enough to lose himself. All those nights of talking with her and his brother came crashing back, of admiring her wit and beauty and finding some vicarious pleasure in seeing his brother so content while ignoring his own attraction. Had he held himself back from wanting her for the entire month?

He happily gave in now. Whether he was in love with her or just the idea of a good solid fuck was beyond his capacity to decide.

His eyes fluttered open long enough to see Alex behind her, naked now and brushing his lips down her neck. Dimitri heard his brother whisper in Thea's ear, "Tell us what you want us to do, love. This is your fantasy."

So that's what this was about. Alex had found a girl he wanted to please badly enough to share. Or maybe it had happened before but this was the first time Dimitri hadn't been spoken for. How the hell was this going to work with the two of them? He'd imagined threesomes before, but those fantasies had always involved indiscriminate sharing of bodies and pleasure. Never had he imagined his brother as the third party. *Focus on her*, he told himself. That was easy enough because she was all over him.

"Lay down on the bed," she said, sending a heated glance at Alex. He obeyed, resting back against her pillows. She turned, darting a coquettish look over her shoulder at Dimitri and gesturing for him to follow. Dimitri's eyes focused on her plump, round ass when she crawled up the bed to his brother. She paused between Alex's legs and dipped her head, slowly taking his cock into her mouth. Alex let out a groan of pleasure and met Dimitri's eyes with a pleased smile. Dimitri knew that look, or at least the inspiration for it, because he'd had it himself on countless occasions. His own cock twitched sympathetically.

Her glistening pussy seemed to lure him in, the bare, lips glistening and slightly parted. *Strawberries*, he thought. His mouth watered and the thought spurred him into motion. He knelt behind her and leaned down, spreading her open for a taste. She moaned around his brother's cock when his tongue slipped into the slick heat. Maybe not strawberries, but she did taste amazing. She made a cute little squeak when he invaded her creamy, wet pussy with two fingers and began fucking into her.

Her head bobbed diligently on Alex's cock. Dimitri watched, easily imagining what her mouth would feel like on him. He and his brother rarely needed words to understand each other. They had never really needed to talk, growing up, somehow reading each other easily through expressions. The intensity of his brother's look wasn't exactly explicit, but it was enough. *Do more*, it said.

Dimitri let his eyes travel over Thea's body. Her plump breasts brushed against his brother's thighs while she worked his cock. He reached a hand down and cupped one, squeezing the tip gently between thumb and forefinger, then rubbing lightly in slow circles. She let out a muffled moan and her pussy clenched around his fingers.

His gaze followed the curve of her spine down to the cleft of her ass. The pink puckered bud of her asshole seemed bereft of attention, so he grazed his thumb across the delicate skin while still thrusting his fingers deep into her.

She moaned and pushed back into his hand. His brother exhaled suddenly and tilted his head back in pleasure.

Dimitri bent his head and trailed his tongue in a slow circle around the tight little opening. She went completely rigid.

"Sorry," he whispered against one pale cheek of her backside.

It was Alex who answered. "Don't stop, oh God don't stop."

Dimitri wasn't sure whether the words were meant for him or for Thea. She stopped in spite of them, and moved away from Dimitri, leaving him kneeling at the foot of the bed, his fingers glazed with her juices.

What had he been thinking trying something like that so soon? He sat there, cock throbbing, trying to decide if he was desperate enough to just jerk off, or if he should get dressed and leave. But he couldn't take his eyes off her now, and neither could Alex. Dimitri envied his brother for that rapt expression. He'd felt the same thing with lovers before, and he felt exactly that when he watched her now. She spread her thighs and straddled Alex's hips. She gripped his twin in one hand and slid the tip of Alex's cock back and forth between her pussy lips. Dimitri rubbed the tip of his own cock with the fingers still wet from her, in an attempt to feel something close to what Alex must be experiencing.

Alex's eyelids fluttered and he let out a long, low sigh when Thea lowered herself onto his cock. Dimitri couldn't tear his eyes away from where they were joined. His hand instinctively gripped his cock and began stroking while he watched her fuck his brother with slow, undulating motions of her hips. She leaned over to give Alex a long, languid kiss. Turning her head to look over her shoulder at Dimitri, she smiled.

"Fuck me, Dimitri. I know that's what you want, so do it. Please, fuck me."

Dimitri blinked, uncertain at first what she meant. He met Alex's fevered gaze briefly and followed his brother's darted glance to the bedside table. What he saw made him immediately feel like a fool. This was what she wanted with them both.

The scent of strawberries wafted to his nostrils when he popped the lid. He squirted a liberal amount of the clear liquid onto his fingertips. As surreal as the evening had been so far, the intensity with which he was able to focus on this particular task overrode every other worry or fear he had up until then. Nothing drove him but the singular desire to feel her coming apart with his cock fucking deep into her ass while his brother worked her from the beneath.

His slick fingertips swirled delicately around her opening. He pressed his index finger at the center, slowly letting it slide in, enjoying how she quivered and buried her face against Alex's neck. She stopped moving her hips, seeming to anticipate what he would do next. Alex kept pumping slowly up into her pussy.

He and his brother locked eyes briefly, holding the gaze while Alex murmured into Thea's ear. "You like that, love? You like my cock deep inside while Dimitri plays with your ass?"

Dimitri shared a smile with his brother, finally enjoying the endeavor without any uncertainty about the implications. If Alex were this comfortable with the idea, there was no reason he shouldn't be, too. And he was invested in seeing Thea fly to pieces once he and his brother were both fucking her. He pressed a second slick digit into her. She cried out and shot her hands out to either side of Alex's head, gripping hard at the pillows.

"Oh fuck that's good," she gasped. Alex turned his eyes to her face, his expression transforming into hungry need. He accepted her rough kiss and reached down to squeeze both her ass cheeks, spreading her wider for Dimitri.

"Now," Alex said.

Dimitri coated his cock with the slick scent of strawberries. Thea whimpered against Alex's lips, then let out a harsh groan when Dimitri pressed his cock against her tight barrier. Alex had slowed his own pace down, only moving with a slow thrust every few seconds. Dimitri's arms quivered with the effort of holding himself poised over her, but he had to go slow.

"Do it!" she commanded through gritted teeth. "Oh God, fuck me. *Please*." Her last word came out as a desperate sob against Alex's shoulder.

Her asshole clenched once around the head of his cock, then relaxed. He slipped in by increments, the tight friction around his cock creating heat like a furnace that coursed through him. He was dimly aware of his own harsh grunts when he finally began fucking her in earnest.

Alex's cock pounded into her again in a frenzy from beneath. Her head thrashed and her hands clawed at the sheets. A long, sobbing moan escaped and her entire body shuddered beneath Dimitri. Her ass clenched tightly around his cock and he abruptly sank into her and stopped, hilt deep, unable to stand it any longer. The pressure of his brother's cock pressed and throbbed beyond the barrier between them. Alex cried out. Or was it Dimitri crying out himself? His throat ached from his own harsh gasps. He panted in time with the surge of his orgasm, the hot stream of his cum shooting deep into her.

When they regained their breath she slipped from between them. She paused long enough to press a kiss against his lips before she disappeared into her bathroom. Dimitri sat back on his heels, dazed and buzzed, though he wasn't quite sure whether it was the remnants of alcohol in his system or from *her*. Thinking perhaps he should leave, he glanced around for his clothes and made a move to get up.

"You'd be an asshole to leave after that," his brother said in a low voice.

Dimitri gave him a questioning look.

"I know you're used to us keeping this part of our lives separate, but it obviously isn't working out for you. Face it, our lives are better when we're both invested in something together. Besides, I'm pretty sure she likes you."

"You think?" Dimitri asked, finally finding the breath to respond.

CHAPTER TWO

"You alright, man?"

Corey's concerned words pulled Dimitri out of the depths of his memories. He'd managed to make a pot of coffee, but now sat in a canvas camp chair ignoring his steaming cup while he stared at the oddly glowing fireplace.

"I'm…yeah, I guess. Being here in this temple feels strange. I always expected if I ever made it to a place like this my brother would be with me."

"You two studied together, right?" Corey asked.

"Yep. He was in Erika's program, but just missed having her for a TA, I guess."

They'd done more than just study together. After that first night with Thea, the sharing of interests even extended to their sex lives. The overlap seemed completely natural once they started, and Thea was more than happy to accommodate both of them. Dimitri had even gone so far as to consider himself content—maybe even truly happy—after six months had passed with the three of them completely inseparable. She fit so well into their lives it was hard to imagine a time when she hadn't been a part of it.

But like his life tended to do, it all fell apart. The red glow of the strange embers in the fireplace became the flashing lights of an ambulance in Dimitri's memory; the waning heat of his mug became the diminishing warmth as his brother's life bled away in the mangled car they were both trapped in. He supposed he should be grateful that Thea hadn't been with them. The aftermath had left his soul as mangled and useless as the heap of metal the emergency crew had pulled him out of. They'd probably tested fate and lost, trying to share Thea's love.

"What would he have said about the dragons, do you think?" Corey asked.

Dimitri took a deep breath and finally sipped at his tepid coffee. "Dragons…" He let out a low chuckle, glad for an excuse to picture the happier image of his brother's enthusiasm over this find. "He'd have loved the dragons. Been totally on board with this whole fantasy world we've discovered down here."

He swallowed his coffee down in a series of quick gulps and poured another cup.

"Where is everyone?" he asked, realizing that most of the sleeping bags were empty. All but Hallie's. She still lay snoring softly like the heavy sleeper she was. Must be nice to sleep with such a clear conscience.

He wondered what it was that had pulled Corey out of sleep. His older friend wasn't exactly the sharing type, so he had no idea what made the man tick. Dimitri had only shared the details of his own life in an effort to try to purge the memories, yet they still haunted him regularly.

That sharing, though, on his part, on many of their parts, had brought the team closer. They were almost a family now, if not quite the one he'd loved and lost. Everyone seemed to bear some kind of burden, spoken or unspoken. Still, knowing he wasn't alone in carrying such pain was a comfort.

"Not sure, but I'm about to go look. Want to join me?" Corey picked up one of his small digital video cameras and set off around the corner. Dimitri followed, happy for the distraction.

Walking through the center of the cavernous main room of the dragon temple, Dimitri thought the place seemed more brightly lit than it had when they'd first arrived. The glowing braziers behind the throne at the far end of the room pulsed in a slow rhythm that he found almost hypnotic.

"Did you ever figure out how the lights work?" he asked.

Corey paused by the throne and glanced around with a concerned look on his face. He shook his head. "Beats the shit outa me. It's driving me nuts that I can't figure it out, though. I was hoping to get Eben's help cracking one open but he's disappeared along with Erika and Camille. Kris is MIA, too."

Dimitri chuckled. "Are you sure you want to go looking? I'll give you three guesses what he and Erika are up to and honestly I don't blame them. Maybe Kris and Camille found a dark corner somewhere, too. If I had a willing partner you can bet that's what I'd be doing right now. A find like this definitely warrants a celebratory fuck."

Corey stooped down and picked something up off the polished jade floor in front of him. He shot Dimitri a critical look. "You guys are probably the most oversexed group of people I've ever had the pleasure of working with, you know that? Except for Camille maybe."

"Sometimes you just need human contact," Dimitri said. "Helps you feel a little less alone in the world."

Corey's expression turned sympathetic. "Yeah, sorry, man. I understand that need, but it's never really worked for me. I need more than just a warm, willing body. I'd rather be alone than screwing a woman I don't feel a deep connection with."

"It's alright. Being here just brought back some old memories. I woke up horny as hell, and all I could think about was that first night Alex and I were both with Thea."

"See, that's not something I could ever see myself doing, either," Corey said. "I guess I'm not the sharing type."

"I didn't think I was either, but it made so much sense once we'd started. I think we were both amazed we hadn't done it before. But I suppose Thea was a special girl. It probably wouldn't have worked with anyone other than her." It had worked, though. Before too long he was as head over heels for her as his brother was. The strangest thing about their relationship was the fact that neither he nor his brother had any reservations about the other's hold on Thea's feelings. And she never once played favorites, which seemed odd to Dimitri since she'd been with Alex first. She became the fulcrum he and Alex balanced their lives upon. Except that after Alex's death suddenly they'd lost their counterbalance and had ultimately spun off in different directions. He'd left finally, after a heart-wrenching argument in which it became apparent she couldn't stand seeing him, being reminded every day of what they'd both lost.

"Check this out," Corey said, handing Dimitri a notebook, the top page halfway filled with Camille's tiny, meticulous handwriting. Dimitri flipped back a few pages and read.

"What the hell?" He stared down at the characters carved into the floor around the base of the throne. "Do you think they're crazy enough to try doing this…this *ritual*?"

"Knowing Erika, yeah," Corey said. "Looks like someone managed to open one of the doors back there. Let's go find them."

Dimitri flipped to the next page and read, enthralled by the very idea that this was even possible. Six phases to the ritual, Camille's translation said. Six members of their group, not counting their guide. *Alex, you would have been all over this.* He noted one of Camille's tiny notes in the margin that said, "What if dragons are real?!" in one spot. When he reached the last page, he found an underlined section of text in a language he didn't understand, with another note written in English off to the side, "No wonder we're all so worked up in here. It's by design. It takes *nirvana* to wake one up. Nirvana equals orgasms?"

He tossed the notebook back down where Camille had left it and jogged to catch up with Corey. His mind processed the possibilities presented in Camille's notes. The other man was probably too pragmatic to believe it, but Dimitri had a surge of hopeful excitement. This just confirmed what he and his brother had speculated. He'd accepted Erika's invitation to join the expedition for the novelty more than anything, but now it seemed there were facets to this place that were beyond his wildest dreams.

The giant pair of carved jade doors loomed in front of him, one pushed open just far enough to allow a person to pass through. Corey, ever the diligent cameraman, hit the on switch and began recording as he went.

"You first," Corey said, gesturing for Dimitri to enter.

The wide hallway curved around, mimicking the rear arc of the dais the throne sat upon in the main chamber. Five large doors were spaced at intervals along the apex of the arc, the central door much larger than the other four.

The door closest to them stood open, and from the sounds that emanated from inside Dimitri had the oddest sense that he was walking onto the set of a porn movie.

He glanced back at Corey, gave his friend a smirk and opened his mouth to say, "I told you so." "Except the moment he turned, he found himself close enough to get a first peek into the room itself. The smirk disappeared and the words caught in his throat. He stopped dead in his tracks, his jaw dropping open at the completely unexpected tableau that greeted him.

"What is it?" Corey asked, looking up from the digital display on the back of the camera.

"See for yourself," Dimitri said.

He felt a little wrong watching them, but found it difficult to tear his eyes away. They were tangled up in groups of three. He recognized Camille and Eben in one trio. Their companion was a magnificent man with pale skin, long white hair and horns. Camille straddled his lap, riding on the man's cock like she was born to fuck him in spite of the shy confession of her virginity that Dimitri had pried out of her the week before. Eben knelt beside the couple, locked into a passionate kiss with the man.

Dimitri's eyebrows shot up at this scene. He'd always suspected Eben's more universal sexual tendencies, but this was the first confirmation he'd had.

Across the room a similar scene played out, with Erika and two other unfamiliar figures, both with vibrant sheens to their skin and similar curved protrusions on their heads. Who the hell were these people? *Creatures…Dragons…*He could almost hear Alex's voice rejoicing in his mind when the scope of what they had discovered down here occurred to him.

Erika lay languid across the lap of a red-haired man while a violet-horned woman knelt between her legs, attending to her. Dimitri watched, fascinated, while they changed places. Erika went down on the other woman while the red man positioned himself behind Erika.

In a previous life Dimitri might have announced himself and asked to be included, but now he just stood enthralled. Alex would have loved the opportunity to be a part of this. The only thought in Dimitri's mind was that this was only one room out of dozens. He wanted his own dragon.

He turned to express this thought to Corey but shut his mouth before the words could sneak out. Corey stood completely rigid and not at all entertained by the scene. His jaw flexed, no doubt grinding his teeth hard enough to lose a layer of enamel…the man was too tense in general.

The sounds in the room escalated. Then before their eyes, the three exotic newcomers shifted almost in unison, as if they had some shared cue when they orgasmed. Suddenly the previously human-looking figures became mythical, beautiful things with wings flaring wide and elongated faces spouting colored smoke and resonant cries of pleasure. Red and white and lavender. Dimitri found it difficult to stop watching until Corey cursed and walked away, leaving Dimitri staring wide-eyed. He thought the dragons would be bigger, but that didn't mean they were any less impressive.

He wanted to be a part of this ritual so badly the wanting made him numb to the hard throb between his thighs. Logically it made no sense, but his compulsion spurred him on and he went with it, moving to the next door in the row. The closed door stood there, the shining gold surface of it glowing at him with subtle, tantalizing pulses of light.

The door. Camille's notes had detailed the importance of these particular doors. Each one represented a new phase of the ritual. Each one required a unique personality to open it and her notes speculated that their group had the perfect combination to see the ritual through.

He paused and stared at the thing. Tried to be analytic about it. From an anthropological standpoint, it was a curiosity. Dragon worship wasn't unheard of, but what culture was so beast-centric to depict humans in coitus with reptiles? *Dragons, just like Alex and I always believed.* The thought sent a thrill through him, but he tried to process the information objectively anyway. In the Western world it would've been seen as Satan worship, no doubt. But in the context of what he'd witnessed a moment ago he believed there had to be more to it than mere worship.

They'd looked human at first. Super-human, really, but still recognizable and articulate creatures. The red-haired one was particularly vocal and there was no mistaking how much he'd been enjoying giving it to Erika for all he was worth. And she was every bit as vocal back to him. Fuck, had that been a turn-on.

But the more he stared at the golden image carved into the door, the less it mattered. He stepped closer and raised a hand to trace the figure of one of the two dragons that flanked the human. When his fingertips came into contact with the surface, a jolt of pure, electrical pleasure shot through him.

"Are you crazy?" Corey asked. Dimitri jerked back from the door as though he'd been caught with his hand in a cookie jar.

"I'm going in," he said.

"The hell you are." Corey gripped him by the shoulder. Dimitri pulled away, frustration churning in his stomach, beginning to condense in a hot ball of spite at being held back. Before he could retaliate another figure joined them.

"Let him go in," Kris said in a soft, measured voice. "He's meant to open that door. You see the twins there?" Kris pointed at the raised figures on the door's golden surface.

Corey gave the door a cursory glance. "I call bullshit," he said. "You slipped some drug in our dinner last night. Now we're all hallucinating."

Kris shook his head. "I won't deny this is a powerful place, but all I've done is help guide you all to where you already belong. Dimitri belongs inside that room."

"What happens once I go in?" Dimitri asked.

"You'll have a choice to make. One twin or the other. When you give your nirvana to him or her, and the dragon returns the favor, you will be bonded to that dragon. The power of your union will help to fill the Queen's well. Then, when the time comes, she will awaken and call the rest of the brood to the skies."

"And then what? They take over the world?" Corey asked in a bitter tone.

"No. It's a symbiotic relationship dragons have with humans. Your kind is rarely aware of us. Only those bonded to us know."

"What the fuck do you mean *us*? Are you one of them?"

Kris smiled and nodded. "I'm a pure blood. I'm the conduit through which they will feed all their collected power to the Queen." He turned to look at Corey. "You should prepare yourself, my friend. There are only two of you left, after Dimitri, and you're the only one suitable to be the Queen's mate."

"Let me guess…she likes to bite off the heads of men after she's done with us, right?"

"You know, Corey," Dimitri interjected, "I liked you at first, but now you're just being an obstinate asshole."

"You're the delusional one. I don't know what Kris did to us, but I don't believe this magical dragon bullshit."

"Fine. You go on not believing it. I'm going to see for myself."

CHAPTER THREE

Five hundred years might seem like a long time to sleep. To Aurin, it was maybe a little too short. Her consciousness aroused for the first time in half a millennium and her first thought was to hope it would go away and leave her be. Let her sleep and fall back into the endless dream of flying—of spreading her wings and casting her large shadow across the earth for days without fatigue or hunger. She could happily fly forever. But the vibrations in the air around her conveyed the fact that it was time. A second later her brother's thoughts invaded her mind, echoing her own.

"It's time, Sister."

"Yes, Aurik. I sense it. Now we wait."

"It won't be long. Humans are impatient creatures."

The velvet blanket of darkness still covered them. Until their part of the ritual began she was still blind and paralyzed. She recalled the ritual to send them all to sleep. Each new generation of their race was sent into a magical stasis to mature while the prior generation lived out their long lives among humans. Five hundred years had passed in the blink of an eye. With a surge of sadness she understood that their awakening meant the last of the prior generation had finally been committed to the skies for eternity. A dragon's death was rare enough that it made the awakening bittersweet to know that she and the other members of the new generation would be cast into the world soon, with only the memories of their parents' teachings to guide them.

Her brother was close enough to touch. They'd been frozen like statues, back-to-back with scant inches between them. Frozen in their human forms as the ritual dictated. Only the guardians and the Shadow were allowed to keep their dragon forms in sleep. Their defenders had to be ready to protect them. The other members of the dragon court slept in their human forms, as did the dozens of other dragons that slumbered within the sanctuary of the temple along with her. Her brother didn't mind it so much, but it made her itch.

"They're taking too long," she griped.

"They'll take as long as they need to. Issa will know when to urge them on, though. We're second."

"Hmm…I wonder what he'll be like. Remember mother telling us how her first chosen had no idea what to do with her? He was a Sultan, even. She said he was terrified when she changed. I hate coercing men into sex, even if they do love it. Sometimes they're so needy afterward."

"It may be a woman who comes in. Whoever it is, they will have to choose between us. You know this."

She seethed inwardly at being reminded of the strict laws they had to adhere to, one of which was that no human should have dominance over two dragons. Except whoever awakened them would be *their* property, not the other way around. Added to that was the even more distressing law that dictated dragons must travel alone until the first of the new brood was born. Too many dragons sharing a border could cause conflict. The old council feared their competitive, greedy natures would result in wars. In spite of her certainty that she and Aurik would be well behaved, she wondered if the laws would even allow them to stay together.

"I'd rather share with you than be parted. I don't want you to have to go find your own mate alone."

"And what a hopeless search that would be, too. Women bore me. I'll make you a promise, Sister. If it is a man and we both take to him, we make a pact to let him wake us both, and we share. If it is a woman, I'll make do with her, but vow that I will stay as near to you as possible until you find your human mate."

"But will the Queen even allow it?"

"Every cycle presents new complications, Sister, resulting in new laws. Maybe we can make the argument and be heard. Patience."

Bolstered by her brother's certainty that sharing the man who awakened them would be possible, she turned her mind to contemplation of what he might be like. Different than the human men she'd known before sleeping, she hoped.

"Do you hear that?" Aurik asked, eagerness obvious in his voice.

She trained her ears to the sounds outside. Voices spoke beyond their door.

One insistent, accented voice said, "It's my choice, Corey. I believe it. You saw the others with your own eyes."

A gruffer voice replied, "Dimitri, there's no proof. You're a *scientist*. You know better."

"No proof? They fucking *changed right in front of you*. Dragons! If you can't believe your eyes, what can you believe?"

The other voice grumbled, "I believe we've been drugged and the rest of you are too in love with Erika's fantasy to see the truth. It's all one big hallucination."

"Fine, you believe that if you want, but I have blue balls from hell right now so I'm willing to do just about anything to fix that."

"Just find a dark corner. I'll look the other way."

"Christ, Corey! Don't you think I've tried that? Something's *different* about this place. You go find a dark corner and try it, why don't you."

"What are blue balls?" Aurin asked her brother.

"I can only guess, but I suspect he's sexually frustrated."

The air released in a sudden rush when the door opened, breaking the seal of the room they'd been contained in. If she'd been able to move, her skin would have quivered in response to the gust. She could smell *him*, at least. Male musk and sweat and an underlying sweetness that she recognized as goat milk. But the aroma was subtle, like he'd been fed on it as a child. He smelled of the old world she was accustomed to. Was this really the time? Surely it couldn't have been five hundred years already if the man who came to wake them smelled so familiar.

"Do you smell him?" she asked her brother.

"Yes, Sister. If I weren't already hard as polished jade, I would be now."

She couldn't laugh or roll her eyes at her brother, but knew exactly what he meant. She was aroused by this new man's scent.

For the first time she cursed the darkness that surrounded her. They could hear and smell …they could communicate silently with each other as always. But they couldn't see or touch or taste anything.

A few seconds later she realized that was no longer true. As is soft footsteps approached, the closer he came the more her hard jade skin began to tingle, until it felt alive for the first time in centuries. He paused close enough for the heat radiating off his body to warm her. The temperature change in such close proximity sent invisible shivers down her skin and the alluring scent of him grew even stronger. Oh, sweet Mother, she wished she could see him.

The slow caress of a warm finger down her naked arm was enough to send her shattering to pieces if she really were only polished jade and not a living thing inside a prison.

"Oh."

"Did he touch you, too?"

"Yes."

Then the most astounding thing happened. He started talking in a low, smooth voice. At first she didn't understand the words as she had the ones he'd spoken earlier, but within a second or two she caught up to the nuances and her mind filled in the rest. He spoke Greek, but a dialect far removed from the last time she'd heard it spoken. His cadence and inflections teased at her ears. When he finally stopped talking she wished he would begin again.

"I wish I knew your names. You are too beautiful for words. I don't quite know what I'm supposed to do, but it seems like such an intimate thing that I shouldn't just start trying to fuck you." He laughed, the sound tickling her ears. "Like that's even possible…I mean, you're *statues*. But you're really more than that, aren't you? Corey doesn't believe in this supernatural nonsense. Neither do I, really, but evidence is evidence. And I don't feel drugged. Fuck, you are both so beautiful."

He paused and traced a finger down her cheek. She could have wept from the tender contact if she'd been able to. But the sensation was stark and jarring against stone skin that had been numb for centuries. She could *feel* him now.

"I want to wake you up," he continued. "But I have no idea how. Camille's notes say I need to give one of you my nirvana. Is she right about the sexual aspect of it? Is that why you're both naked and ready? Well, at least one of you is ready."

She heard a frustrated huff expel from his mouth, and a warm gust of air brushed past her face. His breath smelled of curry and dragon magic.

"In fairy tales, it works with just a kiss, maybe that's enough."

She heard nothing but his heartbeat as close as he was, and the brush of skin against stone somewhere behind her.

"He's kissing you, isn't he?" she asked.

"Oh yes. Sweet he is, Sister." Her brother's voice sounded elated.

"Damn you."

But she didn't carry her envy for long because a moment later the same warm lips pressed against her rigid, unresponsive ones. If any kiss could have awakened a sleeping princess, his would have done the trick. But she was no princess, nor was her brother. It took more than a kiss for them. Still, she strained within her prison to respond to the sweet, soft press of his lips. The warmth of his flesh left her tingling even deeper when he pulled away with a sigh.

"Not enough, huh? I guess this is a different fairy tale."

She heard soft swishing sounds. His movement pushed wafts of his scent to her nose. She guessed he was undressing, and oh how she wished she could see him. A man with a scent like that and lips that kissed so well *must* be lovely to look upon.

"I should tell you both something before I wake you up. I don't know if you can even hear me…but I need to say this anyway. Kris said I had to choose between you. But there's no way in hell I can do that. I don't know how this…ritual works, but he's told me enough. I know deep inside that you two are going to save my life. That's why I'm doing this in spite of my logic telling me it's crazy. If you *do* wake up after this then I'll know the truth. If you don't then I guess I just hope I've found some peace to move on."

Something warm pressed against the rigid curve of her breast. His fingertips brushed around the heavy swell, curling up to trace the outline of her nipple. She felt every single increment of the contact as though each cell of her being were sending its own cries of gratitude at the contact to her soul.

Another part of her reacted to the contact, too, and it felt so real it ached. The tight bundle of nerves between her thighs felt like it contracted and she wished she could touch it to see if it were awake. She needed to know whether they were just phantom sensations of wetness or if they were real. The sensation magnified when his warm touch grazed the tip of her other breast.

But he stopped touching her. She sensed him moving, facing away toward her brother. She wanted to yell out but wasn't yet able to speak. She could only listen to the brief sounds that her hyper-sensitive hearing picked up. Sounds like she'd heard when he touched her, skin on stone, caressing in adoration.

"Yes, he is the one," Aurik said in a languid voice a moment later. *"I almost regret my offer to share, but I will."*

"What did he do to you?"

"Enough to let me know."

CHAPTER FOUR

Dimitri let his hand skitter off the end of the golden statue's erect cock. The warmth of it still tingled on his skin, a subtle signal to him that there was more to these statues than Corey believed. And these two…they were posed so perfectly. Back-to-back, identical aside from their obvious genders. The translucent gold of the jade they were made from shimmered in the flickering lights, enticing him to touch them both more. And he would, because he couldn't resist. The few soft caresses he'd given them earlier had only incited deeper cravings. Cravings that didn't help the aching in his balls while he stared at the two of them. To choose would be impossible. He had to find a way to awaken them both.

"You are two halves of a whole. That's why I have to wake you up together. You see, I was like you. A twin. But I lost my other half last year. And I…" His breath caught in his throat and he paused to stare into the female's stone eyes, imagining she could see him and was looking back with understanding. "I lost myself after my brother died. Ever since, I've been carrying around this dark emptiness that's slowly eating me alive." The only times he'd managed to come close to finding peace after Alex's death and Thea's withdrawal were the random, pointless hookups he'd made late at night with near strangers. They proved ultimately too fleeting and empty of meaning.

Standing beside these two figures, for the first time since that first night with Thea and Alex, his life felt pregnant with possibility. If he could awaken two creatures like these beautiful dragons, find that apex of peace together, he might just be okay. Even if it were only one encounter, he believed he could leave here closer to whole than when he arrived.

His hands kept steadily trailing over the surface of their jade skin. Up the male's arms, down his lean, sculpted chest, then switching his attention to the female's sweeping swell of breasts, the heft of which he could feel in his palm even though they were made of rigid mounds of stone tipped with hard little peaks. He experimentally bent his head to one, teasing the smart tip with his tongue. The texture of it was so close to real it caused a tingle to travel down his spine, and his balls tightened. He was sure he could hear a sigh from somewhere in the room, but when he looked at her placid face nothing had changed.

Both were nearly the same height as him, and slender but well-built. They were completely nude, with long, wavy tresses carved from the same jade, draping in perfect thick tendrils over their shoulders. The male also had the hint of a goatee decorating his angular face.

He circled them, touching by increments as he went, marveling at the warm, smooth texture of their skin. He paused in front of the male once and leaned in for a kiss. The lips felt smooth and he could almost imagine how pliant and inviting they'd be were the man alive. His tongue tingled when he grazed it lightly in the crease between, over the barely visible hint of teeth. He let his hand slide down the front of the figure's torso and come to rest on the rigid cock that jutted from between the golden thighs. It felt warmer now. He must be imagining it…it must be warmth from his nearness permeating the stone. Still, it felt so close to life-like, rendered in minute detail from the sparse texture of carved thatch at the base to the tiny ridges of veins and the slight upward curve. The entire magnificent arc capped by the most delicious looking head, slightly tapered from the thicker shaft.

He stroked it in one long, languid motion, gripping his own cock in his fist at the same time. His living flesh jerked against his palm and a tiny moan escaped his lips.

"Fuck. I'd love to be sandwiched between the two of you. You're just facing the wrong way right now. So what do you think I should do?"

He slipped back around to face the female and rested his lips against hers now, letting them linger a little longer while his hands traced the curve of her waist and his fingertips trailed up to her breasts. He made tight little circles around her nipples imagining she were alive and responsive.

All he could think was to touch them. Make love to them as best he could, considering they were mute, solid forms, frozen and beautiful.

He began by falling to his knees before her and pressing his mouth into the intricately carved folds between her jade thighs.

CHAPTER FIVE

"Oh, sweet Mother..." Aurin exclaimed.

"Tell me, Sister. Don't hide or I'll be very jealous. What is he doing?"

"Licking me. And he has such a lovely tongue, too."

"That he does. That kiss. I can still taste it. So sweet. And he kissed me first."

"Brother, when he wakes us I'm going to punch you."

Aurik's chuckle vibrated through her mind. *"You might be too busy stroking his cock to worry about payback. How does his tongue feel, Sister? Am I going to like feeling it on my cock?"*

The tongue in question licked between her thighs with a kind of abandon, like she were made of hard rock candy that might melt and not solid stone. The sensations his steady flicks and swirls produced certainly made her feel like melting. Hundreds of years it had been since she'd had a tongue between her thighs. But she knew how the ritual was supposed to work. He had to make a sacrifice to them. His nirvana. If he exhausted himself with his selflessness, that would *not* serve their purposes.

He let out an audible, rumbling groan and she felt his head shift lower, his tongue sinking deeper.

"Oh! Something's happening. Is this supposed to happen?"

"What? Tell me, Sister!"

"I'm...I don't know. I feel like I'm coming alive. My cunt is, at least. But he hasn't sacrificed his nirvana to us yet."

"You've got his tongue in your little dragon snatch and you're complaining?"

"No, you imbecile. You know we won't wake up until he gives it to us."

Her brother began to answer but she grew distracted by the growing heat between her thighs. Something was *definitely* going on down there. The man's steadily moving tongue was splayed across her clit that felt way too alive for how frozen the rest of her was.

"Oh Christ, you're ...you're *wet* and soft, and ...oh shit," he said.

She wanted to scream out, "And what?" and then grab his head and push it back against her. But she couldn't do that. All she could do was itch inside her prison wishing he would get on with pleasuring himself instead of her so she could break out and throw herself on him. Except she didn't want him to *stop* pleasuring her, either. She might come. Would it count, she wondered? Would she even be able to? Oh, sweet Mother, she'd love to find out.

"I...oh shit. Am I allowed to do it first? Is it possible?"

"He's that good, huh? Damn you, Sister. I thought for certain that he'd pick me first."

The string of expletives on her lips fell short when the tongue between her legs was supplemented by a pair of fingers slipping silk-like into the tight crevice of her pussy. They didn't just slide in, though. They pushed against her now very alive pussy walls and he teased at the insides of her while murmuring pleased little sounds against her clit. Sounds like, "Yeah, that's it. My magic fingers just broke your spell, huh?" But the steady finger fucking and gentle tweaking of her swollen nub made her a little deaf to the rest.

"He's in me. Oh. Oh. How…how is it possi- uh."

Her brother had the nerve to giggle over her reaction. She'd have happily breathed fire on him if that were still allowed. She might still do it anyway after she were free. Damn the rules.

"Are you gonna come, Sister? Stuck in this prison?"

She might just do it. That tongue of his was so talented and insistent. She could even feel the pliancy of her pussy under his touch. What would happen if she did come, most of her body trapped in this rigid form?

What he did next solved the problem.

"I'm going to fuck you now, if that's okay. You feel like you're enjoying what I did anyway. I'm no geologist like Eben, but I'm pretty sure rocks don't normally get that soft and wet when you lick them."

"You bitch," her brother's voice intoned in her mind. Like she cared. Her pussy was awake. More than awake, it felt like her entire existence rested right between her thighs in that bundle of swollen, throbbing flesh that had clearly come to life before the rest of her and that he was still stroking and licking. And now he was standing up and pressing the hot tip of his cock to it.

If she could have yelled out she would have.

"Yes, just fuck me!"
"You couldn't help yourself, could you, Sister?"
"Oh, but he feels so good. He's going too slow."

"Describe it to me, please?"

"Oh , Brother, he is thick and so, so sweet. He is so sweet, Brother. This one, if we share him, we must treasure him."

Her brother's chuckles of amusement in her mind faded into the background with the thrust of the human man's cock into her needy pussy.

"Oh, sweet Jesus you feel amazing. Tight and hot," the man said, his warm breath leaving tangible condensation on her jaw. His low, desperate groan resounded in her ears. One of his hands warmed her ass cheek where he held it to gain leverage while he fucked up into her. His other arm reached past her, however.

"Ah, that's nice," her brother intoned from behind her.

"Oh, is he ...?" She was unable to finish her question amid the steady push of the man's cock into her.

"His hand...fingers are...oh yes that is very, very nice."

"I described for you, Brother. Your turn. Tell me!"

"Your description was lacking, ah...but the man's not shy. And not inexperienced. Ohh, God."

She'd have felt a bit giddy hearing her brother's normally collected demeanor so rattled, except that her own was pretty rattled, too. Her pussy felt too thick and full of him. She couldn't make a sound but her mind was busy crying out with every dirty curse she could think of.

"Sister, you just made an unholy noise in my head, what happened?"

"Ah. Shut up."

The truth was that she couldn't even think straight enough to answer. It wasn't enough that the man's beautiful aroma kept sinking into her nostrils, but his perfect cock kept sinking into her pussy, too. And to top it off, her clit had apparently fully melted and the steady rub of his pelvis against it sent jolts of pleasure through her from head to toe. Her ears tingled from the soft little guttural noises he made that bordered on dirty language. Then she realized they *were* dirty words. But the dirty words weren't only about her, they were about her brother, too.

"Fuck, your pussy's so tight, and Christ your brother's ass wants me so bad. I wish there were two of me so I could fuck you both."

The statement startled her.

"Brother?"

"You told me to shut up," he responded smugly. *"Yes…parts of me are a bit more flexible than they were before. The parts he touches. Remind me why we agreed to sleep back-to-back?"*

"The Queen said we had to. He's not supposed to wake us both, but he's going to anyway, isn't he? Yeah, that's nice and I think he might be about to come. Tell me, Brother, does he still have a finger in your backside?"

"Two. And when I'm awake again I'm definitely returning the favor."

"He's decided I need one, too. Like his perfect cock wasn't enough."

"What, a finger in your ass?"

"Oh yes. Oh, sweet Mother, yes."

"Sister, you know I get first crack once we're awake now right? It's only fair if you get him fucking you now and all I get is a couple fingers, not even a cock-grab."

"Uh-huh, fine." That was all she could lurch out between the thrusts, then the man's harsh cries made her ears vibrate, the sensation a refreshing change from all the silence of the past

centuries. To hear the passionate cries of a man was one of the things she'd missed most. Warm heat spread between her thighs. She wished she'd been awake enough to come with him, but there would be time for that soon. Very soon.

An odd popping sounded in her ears as if pressure released, then the world fell out beneath her. The human man's voice echoed around her and with another solid thrust his seed heated her dormant womb. Everything melted into electric clarity. The cool air shocked her skin, the light burned her eyes. But she could *see* the light now, and she could see his lovely face, flushed and exultant after his orgasm.

Wide, blue eyes framed by long, golden lashes stared back at her in amazement.

She wanted to throw him down and fuck him until she reached her own climax, but he was so pretty and shocked to see her eyes blink open, she knew she had to at least give him something. She unfurled her wings first, reveling in the pleasant stretch of long unused muscles. She caught the air with them and wrapped her legs around his hips, careful to avoid letting him slip out of her.

"Don't worry, love. You're mine now. I won't hurt you." She dipped her head to his collarbone and let her animus tongue flick out to mark his skin, worrying that if she waited she'd miss her chance.

"Sister," a deep voice spoke from beside her as her brother's lithe figure moved around behind the man. "Don't forget to share."

CHAPTER SIX

Events bled into themselves after Dimitri came inside the statue's incongruously soft, wet pussy. Two figures rotated around him. He was still standing, his cock solidly sunk inside the woman, but now her legs were wrapped around his hips and she had *wings*. His body tingled with the buzz of pleasure. He'd only hoped for one brief moment of pleasure with one of them. Now that it was done, it hit him that no, this was barely scratching the surface.

Her lips were definitely not light on his own when she kissed him. It was the kiss that finally made him stumble and kneel on the ground, shaky from the orgasm.

"I did it," he mumbled to no one.

"You *did*," a male voice murmured in his ear. A pair of lips brushed against his shoulder, sending delicious tingles through him.

"My sister marked you already, it's my turn. Formality, you understand."

Dimitri cupped the girl's ass and squeezed. The other figure knelt beside him and a strong hand gripped his chin, gently urging him to turn his head. Soft lips fringed with coarse blond hair met his, the man's velvety tongue insistent as he delved between Dimitri's lips. The lips grazed his jaw and lower, until they pressed against his collarbone just opposite where the girl had branded him a second ago.

In the blink of an eye, the figure poised above him wasn't a man, but a golden dragon, forked tongue flicking out and gliding over Dimitri's bare chest.

"You're smaller than I thought," Dimitri murmured in a daze.

The dragon rumbled and a puff of gilded smoke erupted from his nostrils. He leaned forward and flicked his tongue in a pattern on Dimitri's collarbone opposite where the female had made her mark earlier. Another bright sting seared his skin, but the pain faded quickly with a gold breath from the dragon. *This means we're bonded*, he thought. The understanding unburdened him of a great weight for the first time in a year.

"You don't want to see me at full-size," the dragon said. "We like this size. It's manageable. Full size is good for flight and not much else."

"Show me anyway, if it's no trouble," Dimitri said, fascinated to know everything he could learn about these amazing creatures.

"Show him, Aurik." The warm figure of the female shifted to a slightly less intimate position on his lap, but still wrapped herself around him possessively. "My brother is very big. You'll like him," she whispered into Dimitri's ear.

He's big in a lot of ways I like, Dimitri mused, but was still eager to see the dragon. "I'd like to see you, too," he whispered to the girl. He'd learned her brother's name so far, but not hers.

"My name is Aurin," she said as if reading his mind. "What do we call you?"

"Dimitri."

She gave him a sweet, glowing smile. "I'd love to change for you, Dimitri. Anything you like." She pulled away and joined her brother.

Aurik had a wicked expression on his face when she approached him and the scene had the feel of a standoff, the two of them a few paces apart and facing each other. Dimitri sat up to watch.

She slowed and flexed her muscles.

"Biggest wins, Brother?"

"No. He wants to see our natural forms. Honesty, Sister."

She sighed. "Right, okay." She turned to face Dimitri who stared goggle eyed.

The air shifted around him and suddenly two large beasts shared the room with him.

He stood up abruptly.

"Jesus you guys are gorgeous."

Aurik was immense—he took up half the room. He stretched his wings and knocked a vase off a pedestal, then quickly drew them back against his sides. Dimitri walked closer, slid a palm over the dragon's scaled knee. The texture felt like velvet, which was unexpected.

"You guys have fur?"

"Not fur," Aurik said in a rumbling voice. "Just the surface of our scales. Defensive filaments. We're impervious to damage in these forms."

"Oh. It feels nice, though." Dimitri couldn't stop touching it, as soft as it was. He let his hand trail further up Aurik's large thigh. The dragon settled back and a sigh of gold smoke washed over Dimitri.

Curious, he kept stroking further. The taut muscle of the dragon's thigh flexed and his immense cock twitched and pulsed before Dimitri's gaze. It had been nearly two years since he'd been intimate to any significant degree with another man. Each time he tried, he would see his brother's face the last time they had made love to Thea. It often seemed strange to him that he had no qualms about looking in his brother's eyes with Thea's sensuous figure and sounds of pleasure as a buffer between them. But the second she was gone he hadn't been able to touch another man. It just felt wrong without a woman between them. Without Thea.

Now he wanted nothing more than to touch this creature and to be touched by him. He reached out a tentative hand and stroked up the length of the dragon's cock. No velvet armor adorned the beautiful shaft. It was entirely hot, golden skin, the length of Dimitri's arm.

"You can stop me, but I admit I'm curious. Is this as big as you get?" Dimitri asked.

"Not quite, but there's not enough room in here. Particularly not when you're touching me like that." The response was guttural and definitely aroused. "I think you're making Aurin a little jealous."

Dimitri became aware of the other dragon in the room. She raised a ridged brow at him over one golden eye. A plume of shimmering smoke rose from her graceful snout.

"You wanted us both," she said. "Now that you've got us, what are you going to do, Dimitri?"

He looked back and forth between them.

"Ah…do you get off better in this form?"

The siblings exchanged a sardonic look. Aurik answered. "Our form doesn't matter. We change to accommodate our partners."

"Oh, good. As much as I'd love to experience a full-sized dragon cock, you'd probably kill me in the process. I need you *both* and my size seems more manageable."

"Wise plan," Aurik said, his form shimmering to resume a human size and shape.

Aurin seemed reluctant to change.

He stepped toward her where she sat on her haunches a few paces away. She was easily the size of an SUV, but more eager for his touch. He could tell by the short, gusting breaths she let out when he approached her. He remembered that he'd been the only one to come so far.

He reached up a hand to her head.

"You don't need to pet me, but I do like it," she said with humor in her voice.

"Maybe I'll just pet you here," he said. He stroked his palms down her large thighs that were spread before him. The same velvety texture of her golden scales teased at his skin. So soft. Christ he'd never touched anything as soft, not even human skin. It made him wonder what her pussy felt like.

He let his hands keep moving, enjoying the quiver of her muscles under his palms. She liked his touch and the evidence was very apparent the closer he got to her pussy.

A sweep of a tongue grazed his shoulders and he looked up in question.

"Just wanted you to know you're on the right track."

He nodded and moved forward, his eyes on the tight seam of scaled flesh between her thighs. He knew something wonderful waited beyond, and couldn't wait to discover it.

He reached out a tentative hand to graze her slit. All he could see was the faint seam in the center, but it gleamed with wetness. He raised his knuckles to his nose to smell her, then licked, watching her dragon eyes react. A low growl rumbled in her throat and her tongue lashed out.

"You're a tease," she rumbled. "I like it."

"Open up your dragon pussy, baby, let me see what I can do with it."

"It doesn't work that way. You've got to have a cock big enough. But dragons rarely mate with each other anymore, so that's why we change shape most of the time. We're accustomed to being smaller."

"You'd like a big cock that can fill that dragon pussy wouldn't you?"

"No…I want you. I can change my size at will, so I can accommodate any size that would fulfill me."

"Oh? Can you get even bigger?"

A hesitant rumble rose from her chest and she glanced behind him at Aurik. After a second she nodded her large head slightly. The air warmed around him and she stretched her wings. Her large body bunched and tensed, her scales shimmering and stretching.

The space she occupied forced him to move back several steps. He bumped into a warm body behind him and was immediately enveloped in a pair of thick arms.

"You like big? She's almost as beautiful as I am at her full size," Aurik whispered in his ear. She kept growing until she nearly filled the room and her head bumped against the lip of the deep skylight above them. He stared up at her angular head, highlighted from behind by a dark square of night sky and stars.

"You're bigger?" Dimitri asked, marveling at the immense creature before him. He'd never seen anything so beautiful. Her gold scales gleamed and sparkled in the low lights. She could barely stretch her wings in the room even as large as it was. He could have fit five of his childhood homes inside this room alone, and she seemed to occupy every inch of it. Not just with her beautiful dragonesque bulk, but with her presence. She still eyed him with curious amusement, waiting for him to render judgment for her change.

"I'm bigger, yes," Aurik said, emphasizing his words by pulling Dimitri's hips back against his very large and very erect cock.

Dimitri's thick arousal pulsed at the heat of the other man behind him. Aurik's fingertips dug into Dimitri's hips and pulled more deliberately forcing Dimitri's ass cheeks apart so the thick length of his cock pressed between them. Christ it had been so long since he'd had a proper fuck, but tasting Aurin had incited a deep longing for feminine flesh against his mouth as much as he wanted the solid thrust of a cock deep in his ass. Jesus, did it have to be so fucking complicated with him? Nobody had pleased him enough since Alex's death. He'd only sought out the most mindless of encounters, chased that brief pinpoint of pleasure, then left without looking back. For the first time since that day he finally had the desire to find something deeper that might last.

"Be gentle with him, Brother. He looks uncertain." The resonant voice and gust of sweet breath over his skin made him look up at Aurin's majestic form again. Her wings were folded along her back and she'd settled down, remaining in her dragon form. She looked relaxed, but attentive.

"He hasn't objected yet, Sister. But I will take care. Dimitri, your bond to us is more than just a mark on your skin. It means we are obligated to see to your needs, too."

That was an understatement. The care Aurik was currently taking involved a steady, sure stroke of his cock between Dimitri's ass cheeks. No hint of expected penetration at all, but enough friction to make Dimitri want to beg. When he was about to do just that, Aurik's large hands slid over both his hip and gripped his cock in one hand, his balls gently in the other.

"Sister, do you want to have a taste?"

Dimitri opened his heavy eyelids, his heart suddenly pounding in anticipation. That was something he'd never in a million years imagined.

Aurin puffed another cloud of golden smoke from her nostrils and her heavy voice reverberated through the room. "I was going to say no at first, but he looks like he'd like me to. Would you like this big tongue of mine to lick those dainty little balls of yours, sweet thing?"

Dimitri felt as though he might come again at the mere idea and he stared down at his cock as though it were Judas.

Aurik's thumbs slipped up his length slightly, aiming his pointed tip closer to the dragon mouth that had lowered and hovered closer, forked tongue flicking out.

"Oh, God yes," Dimitri said when Aurin's hot tongue met the underside of his cock. She traced the length of him in a slow, wet caress that sent him right back to that razor edge of intense pleasure he'd felt while fucking her, just before he came. The twin forks of a tongue that large were apparently incredibly versatile. He lost control of his legs and gripped onto her horns. Now he was spread across her face, but her tongue kept flicking across his cock and balls.

"That's good. Perfect, really," Aurik said from behind him.

Dimitri felt his ass cheeks part. By dragon tongue or fingertips he wasn't sure, but it was definitely a tongue that slipped between a second later to tease at his tight asshole.

"Oh fuck!"

"He does have a sweet ass, Sister," Aurik said.

Dimitri clutched hard at Aurin's horns and closed his eyes, enjoying the warmth of her soft scales beneath his body. Aurik's very hot, wet tongue teased at his sensitive asshole, delving deeper with delicate thrusts while Aurik spread him apart with a solid grip on each cheek. Aurin's large tongue still lapped with languid licks, each one sending him farther and farther from his grip on sanity.

Dimitri panted, anticipating the moment of clarity just before an orgasm that he always loved.

Dimitri whispered a few words, having no idea if either of them would hear, "I've never felt this close to another human before. I want you both like you couldn't believe."

"That's very good," Aurik said just as he pressed the head of his cock hard against Dimitri's slick ass and pushed it home with an agonizingly delicious thrust.

CHAPTER SEVEN

Aurin could smell Dimitri's lust, but the way his warm weight was sprawled across her head she couldn't do much besides dart her tongue out and tease at his cock. He tasted so good, yet she refrained because it was Aurik's turn right now. As frustrating as it was that her brother got first crack, she still loved being Dimitri's anchor.

She lowered her head slightly at a harsh cry from him and a harder grasp on her horns. Aurik was fucking him well.

Good move, sister, bend him over more. Lick him. Suck him if you can.

Oh, that was a new one. Participating in more than an observational role in her brother's escapades? Or he in hers, she guessed…They were a team, after all, but this was the first time he'd ever invited more direct involvement.

She flicked her tongue out, searching. She knew his legs were spread across her snout, but couldn't see where everything was. First she found Aurik's legs and darted her tongue back in to recalibrate. She had no interest in accidentally tasting her brother.

When she slipped her tongue out again it was with more focus. Close to her mouth and up. Ah, there he was. Smooth sack hanging just below her nose, and a very tasty cock riding between the ridges of her nostrils.

She looped her tongue around his very impressive shaft and pulled, moving her head up minutely at the same time.

His cock slipped right between her lips, rubbing against the front of her teeth.

"Oh Jesus. Oh that's nice."

He hadn't let go of her horns and still stood there getting steadily fucked from behind by her brother, but he had a very odd look, like he'd noticed a missing piece in the scenario but it hadn't quite caught up to him.

"No, baby, I want to make you feel good, too," he finally said.

She took his meaning immediately. The changing was a chore, and sapped her energy, but it was always smooth enough. Condensing and transferring energy was all it took. Anything leftover sat in her well for emergencies. In her true form she could draw from the earth, but in this form she could only draw from the residual energy left behind after the change. It rarely mattered in these situations, so she was happy to give him what he asked for. He wanted to fuck her. He *wanted* her. That on its own made her want him even more.

His pretty face was already flushed when she shrank back down to her human form. Aurik's hands gripped his hips so tightly she could see the indentations of her brother's fingertips in Dimitri's tanned flesh.

She lay down, beckoning to him.

Aurik released him, slipping out of his ass with a sigh. Dimitri knelt between her thighs.

"You were beautiful like that," he said, sliding his hands up her thighs in a motion that mirrored what he'd done when she'd shown him her true form. She liked being smaller than human men during sex, though, because they could touch so much more of her. "You still are beautiful, and this way I get to taste your pretty pussy again."

She tilted her head back and let him push her thighs wider. When his hands reached the apex of their journey she felt his thumbs graze over her wet lips and spread them apart. She expected a solid thrust into her, but instead she got a tongue. A slick, agile lick began at her tight asshole and continued through the flooded channel between her pussy lips. There was a reason she loved being human. There were so many more little parts to be touched, and human fingers were so small and adept, equipped to tease.

He circled his tongue lightly around her clit. The wet heat of his mouth against her drove her wild. After a second he paused and looked back behind him.

Irritated at the interruption she followed his gaze to see her brother standing and watching, steadily stroking his own cock.

Before Dimitri could speak, she said, "He wants you to fuck him, Brother. Why are you just standing there with your silly prick in your hand?"

Aurik blinked at her and dropped his hand.

"I didn't want to interfere," he said.

"Well, get used to interfering. We're keeping him, and we're sharing him."

Aurik knelt behind Dimitri and ran a large hand down his back. Dimitri's blue eyes closed and his entire body quivered at the contact. Aurin smiled at the look of pure bliss on Dimitri's face when her brother bent down and flicked his forked tongue out to swirl around and around between their pretty human's ass cheeks. Dimitri sank his head down to rest against her belly, leaving his ass high in the air, spread and ready for Aurik and whatever he had to give. So trusting, so eager. Yet so attentive when he flicked his tongue out and began teasing at her wet and hungry cunt again. She lost interest in what her brother was doing, too enthralled by the very talented tongue working between her thighs. He held her pussy lips apart and drew her between his lips, sucking the sweet little bundle of flesh until she began to shake. Then he stopping and licked gently, teasing and drawing it out.

"Will you turn around?" he asked in a hoarse whisper. "I want to fuck you, but…" He glanced over his shoulder at Aurik whose hand was lost somewhere between Dimitri's ass cheeks, busy enough to make the poor man flush and squirm.

Aurin smiled, understanding. He couldn't compromise the very pleasurable position he was in just now by laying on top of her.

"One condition," she said. She enjoyed the drugged look of acquiescence he had on his face.

"Whatever he's doing to you, if you like it, I want you to do it to me. I want to know what you like."

His thick, hard cock lurched between his thighs. She wasn't sure if it was what she'd asked or something her brother did that caused it, but she didn't care. She wanted him fucking her in whatever way he chose to do it.

She turned around to rest on her hands and knees and thrust her ass back against him, urging him to follow through.

"What's he doing to you, baby? Show me."

A desperate groan met her ears and he gripped both her hips with his hands, pushing her forward slightly. She closed her eyes, waiting to find out what he would do next. Strong fingertips sunk into the flesh of her ass and spread her cheeks wide. A hot gust of air hit her puckered asshole, making it tighten and tingle just before his hot tongue probed and swirled.

"Oh, is that what he's doing to you right now? Do you like that?" she asked, only to receive a muffled response accompanied by another puff of hot air against her ass followed by a low groan. He pulled away for a second, then resumed with fervor, squeezing her ass harder and thrusting his tongue past her tight barrier. The sensation wasn't unwelcome but still made her gasp in surprised pleasure.

She stretched an arm back behind her, threading the fingers of her hand through his hair and urging him to keep going with a gentle push. She didn't remember having a lover quite so eager or versatile. Or so sweetly curious about her nature. It warmed her to her core to feel such acceptance as opposed to the cautious fear she'd experienced during the time before she'd slept. There was, of course, something even more warming about having a talented tongue thrusting into her ass that made the whole situation even more delicious. Her pussy was ripe and dripping with juices now, so thick with arousal it felt like a hard knot of flesh between her thighs, but she was patient.

Her patience was rewarded a second later when he shifted a skittering palm up her side and cupped her breast, tweaking her nipple hard enough to make her cry out, but the sharp bite of pain was tempered by his tongue slipping down between her thighs and thrusting into her wet snatch, teasing at her swollen clit, then moving back to resume licking at her ass.

She no longer cared whether he was mirroring what her brother was doing to him. Not that her brother could've been doing *that* anyway. Nor thrusting a pair of fingers deep into her pussy while his tongue swirled around her tight, puckered asshole. Dimitri still seemed to be trying to honor her request, though. Every few minutes he'd pause and switch, tonguing her ass one second, then biting her ass cheeks, then stroking her clit. Then the pair of fingers he'd been fucking her soaking pussy with slid up and prodded tentatively at her tight opening. When she pushed back he moaned and let them slide in.

"Oh God you're tight," he murmured.

"Are his fingers in your ass, too? Tell me, baby. Do you like that?"

"Uh huh. Oh fuck it feels nice. It all feels so fucking amazing. I want to fuck your ass so hard you scream. Can I fuck you now or do I have to wait for him?"

She bit her lower lip hard, trying to resist an overeager response. She might just fall in love with this lovely human man. So considerate, but so eager. She should make him wait just a little, but oh, did she want exactly what he did.

"You may fuck me, but fuck my wet cunt first. Make sure my juices are coating you well enough before you fuck me my tight netherhole."

"But I'm too big, I think. I don't want to hurt you."

Her heart swelled just a little more at that.

"No, sweet thing, you won't hurt me. I *want* that thick cock inside me. The lubrication is to make it better for you. Go on, fuck my pussy with it."

He obeyed, pressing the tip against her and sliding in. Oh, sweet Mother did he feel good, so hot and hard. Once he was solidly seated deep inside, he even gave a hard little push, just to be sure. But that might have been a result of whatever her brother was doing back there, judging from the harsh grunt that had accompanied it.

He gripped her hips and began fucking, resuming the fingering of her ass with one hand while he moved. Soon she became lost, the pleasure of his cock rubbing against all the sensitive places inside her, sending a myriad of tiny jolts straight to her brain. The sheer pleasure made the room all fuzzy.

He let out a deep groan and paused, his cock pulsing against her pussy walls. His fingers departed from her ass and he slipped out of her pussy, sliding his slick, swollen tip between her ass cheeks and pushing. She pushed back, urging him deeper, relaxing against his steady pressure until his thick length stretched the ring of tight muscle and penetrated her fully. They both sighed when he slid deep in. Another little lurch drove him even deeper and he grunted again. He leaned across her back much the way he'd prostrated himself over her head when Aurik had been fucking him earlier, but this time she knew she would get to come finally. And she was very close.

"Aurik," Dimitri gasped in a harsh whisper. "Oh fuck, yeah. Fuck my ass like that."

She had the same sentiment, but was too far gone to articulate it. Now that he was spread across her back with his hands slipping alternately across her breasts and between her thighs nothing else mattered.

He found her clit somehow in the midst of his own grunts and desperate rutting into her backside. All it took was a steady little rub against the hypersensitive bundle, coupled with a tweak of one nipple and she might as well have been flying again, for the first time in centuries. Yet flying had never felt quite *that* good.

CHAPTER EIGHT

Dimitri regained consciousness amid a tangle of limbs and long golden hair. If there was ever a Heaven he was sure he'd died and ended up there. He lay on his side, one tousled golden head rested against his dead left arm. He looked down expecting to see Aurin, but the incongruous press of soft breasts into his back confused him. No, that was Aurik with his cheek and drooling mouth plastered against Dimitri's skin. Dimitri smiled at the undignified presence, so far removed from the regal dragon he'd seen earlier.

He glanced down past Aurik's head to where the dragon's hand clutched his cock in a loose grip. He felt his flesh tingle and grow taut under Aurik's hand. Before they'd collapsed into a blissful, exhausted sleep he remembered the two dragons laying claim to different body parts of his.

"I want his tongue," Aurin had said.

"Then I want his cock," Aurik replied.

"I want all of you both, all the time," Dimitri interjected. He grinned to himself remembering the stunned expressions they'd given him.

"You can't own us," Aurin said.

"No? Then you can't own me, either. But if you want to, I'll gladly sign a contract, but there's no divvying up of body parts, alright? It makes me feel like you want to slaughter me for meat."

They'd both looked contrite and apologized, reassuring him that they had no intention of eating him. They only intended to fuck him. Then Aurin had given him a wicked little smile and caressed the medallion-shaped tattoo she'd etched into his collarbone. He'd already forgotten about the tattoo along with the matching one Aurik had given him. Brands were what they were, really. They did own him. Body and soul. And the knowledge was frankly transcendent. He no longer felt like he was drifting, lost in the ether without Thea's love or his brother's balance to give his life weight.

The slack hand around his cock tightened and he gasped. Looking down, he saw Aurik's goateed face gazing up at him with suggestive yellow eyes.

"You feel ready again," Aurik observed. The dragon shifted lower, his muscular figure sliding down Dimitri's thigh. He ran his lips along the length of Dimitri's cock, the journey fascinating Dimitri almost as much as the sensation of smooth, warm lips against his cock. Butterflies. Oh fuck that was what he was thinking? He tilted his head back with a groan while the butterflies flitted around his cock. Then Aurik flicked his velvety forked tongue over the tip and Dimitri was reminded of the truth. Dragon tongue. As if butterflies were better? He needed better fantasies.

"Oh, that's nice. What else can you do with that tongue?"

The figure behind him stirred and Aurin slipped her arm around to caress his chest.

"Hmm, I have a tongue too. What do you want, sweet thing?"

His insides melted at the sight of Aurin's sleepy look. Her golden eyes looked expectantly at him from puffy lids visible through a fringe of tangled blond hair.

"You want to make me feel good?"

"Yeah," she said, her voice sexily hoarse in a way that made his cock twitch under Aurik's tongue. God, could he ask for what he wanted? Hell, he'd try it. All she could do was say no, right?

"Do to me what your brother did before."

Her eyes lit up and that was the thing that sent him over completely. There was nothing he wouldn't do for these two if he had to. Especially not now, with her tongue torturing his ass enough to make him shove his cock deep into Aurik's throat.

No. He was pretty solidly in love with the both of them. Aurin's tongue in his ass had a little to do with it. Any girl willing to do *that* on a first date was a keeper. And Aurik had done it first. More than that, he finally felt balanced again, but in a weird way maybe his life had nothing to do with balance anymore. Maybe with them he was the fulcrum. The realization let him relax and give in. He came hard in Aurik's mouth with Aurin still shoving her tongue into his ass.

Released from the burden of grief, now he had a new burden. He looked back and forth between the two dragons. They'd just pleasured him, but were obviously eager for a return favor, which he would give them both.

But just as he reached for Aurin and had his hand about her thigh everything went utterly dark.

Nothing moved, not even the three of them. All Dimitri heard was a whisper of movement. Aurin and Aurik moved away from him leaving him cold and alone.

He heard soft words nearby. "The Shadow's door is open."

"Aurin, is that you?"

The girl's warm flesh slipped into his arms in the dark.

"I'm here," she said, caressing his cheek to comfort him.

"Who's the Shadow?" he asked.

"He's our brother," they said in unison.

"You don't sound excited about that. I'm guessing this means someone…" he paused, remembering what Kris had said to Corey before he'd opened the door. If Corey was meant for the Queen that left one member of their party unaccounted for. "This means Hallie just opened the door. Is she safe with this… Shadow person?"

"Oh, he won't hurt her," Aurin said.

"No," Aurik said. "But I hope she likes dragons with dark moods."

"I take it he's not a glowing, golden beauty like you two?"

Aurin shuddered. "Kol is the exact opposite of us. The only dragon who rebelled against the slumber, so the council made him our keeper."

"And that means what?"

Aurik answered. "It means he's been awake the entire time, his Shadow patrolling the temple for five centuries keeping watch over us. He's probably gone crazy by now."

"It would drive me crazy," Aurin said.

"Do we need to go?" Dimitri asked. Aurin's soft cheek rubbed against his chest when she shook her head. Glowing golden breath erupted from Aurik to the other side of him, casting the three of them in a warm glow for a moment until it dissipated.

"It'll be dark until your friend has completed that phase," Aurik said. "We just need to wait it out, then we go join the others for the next phase."

"Hmm," Dimitri hummed and pulled Aurin tighter. "I heard something about a well that needs filling. How can I help?"

Aurin's lips pressed against his in the dark. Limbs moved around him but he couldn't be sure who was where at first. He felt weightless in the pitch black of the room, drifting off like a lost mote on the breeze. Then her hot wetness sank down onto his hard cock and the muscled length of another hard body slid down beside him. His hand reached out, aimlessly searching until Aurik's hips shifted and his cock pressed up against Dimitri's fingers.

"Thank you," he said softly, unable to find other words to express his gratitude more fully than that, but resolving to return the favor in any way he could until their shared darkness dissipated.

ABOUT OPHELIA BELL

Ophelia Bell loves a good bad-boy and especially strong women in her stories. Women who aren't apologetic about enjoying sex and bad boys who don't mind being with a woman who's in charge, at least on the surface, because pretty much anything goes in the bedroom.

Ophelia grew up on a rural farm in North Carolina and now lives in Los Angeles with her own tattooed bad-boy husband and four attention-whoring cats.

You can contact her at any of the following locations:
Website: http://opheliabell.com/
Facebook: https://www.facebook.com/OpheliaDragons
Twitter: @OpheliaDragons
Goodreads: https://www.goodreads.com/OpheliaBell

Printed in Great Britain
by Amazon